Mummford's® Adventures

Home for the Holidays

ACKNOWLEDGEMENTS

Thank you to my wonderful and talented art team for all your beautiful work.
I couldn't do this without you.
Debbie Mumm

Mummford® is trademarked by Debbie Mumm®
© 1999 by Debbie Mumm
All rights reserved.
Printed in China.

10 9 8 7 6 5 4 3 2
ISBN: 1-890621-33-1
Published by Landauer Books
12251 Maffitt Rd., Cumming, Iowa 50061

www.debbiemumm.com

On a cold December morning in Igloo Village, Elderberry called everyone together. Sounding very serious, he said, "As you all know, Mummford and McFinn have been gone a long, long time. I am afraid they must be lost."

Mummford and McFinn's mother Mummushka said, "I am so worried about my little penguin boys. The holidays are almost here. If Mummford and McFinn don't come home in time, the holidays just won't be the same. Isn't there something we can do?"

Elderberry said, "Can we do something? Why, yes indeed, we can! We can send out a search party. We all want to be together for the holidays, so the sooner we find our friends, the better. Now, are there any volunteers?"

Before anyone else could say a word, Flake and Crystal trotted up to Elderberry. Elderberry smiled. "It's very kind of you to offer," he said, "but I think this job is too big for puppies."

"We may be young, but we are brave," said Flake.

"And we are strong," said Crystal. "We can run like the winter wind."

Elderberry thought for a moment. "This task will not be easy, but I think you are ready to try."

One hour later, Flake and Crystal were ready to go. At the last minute, Mummushka gave them a package wrapped in brown paper tied with string.

She said, "Here is a little something I want you to take on your journey, but you must promise that you will open it only in an emergency." Flake and Crystal promised.

As everyone waved goodbye, Elderberry called out, "Try to be back in time for the holidays." Then they started off across the snowfields.

The sled made a whooshing sound as Flake and Crystal pulled it over the snow. Soon Igloo Village was far behind them.

When they stopped to rest, Crystal looked around. She said, "The world is so big, how will we ever find two little penguins?"

"Well," said Flake, "since Igloo Village is on the South Pole, that means that Mummford and McFinn must be somewhere north." So off they went, heading north.

The trail led into steep mountains. Flake and Crystal dug their paws into the snow and pulled with all their might. Halfway up, Flake said, "Look out!" The sled was slipping off the trail. Crystal threw her weight into the harness, saving the sled in the nick of time.

Flake said, "For a minute, I thought we would have to open our emergency package."

"Me too," said Crystal, "but we did just fine on our own."

The next day was a littler warmer. The two huskies came to a frozen river.

"Now I wish it were a little colder," said Flake. "Do you think the ice is safe?"

"I have an idea," said Crystal as she got out some rope. "I'll lead.
You come in the middle, and the sled will follow at the end."

Step by step, the two huskies made their way across the river.

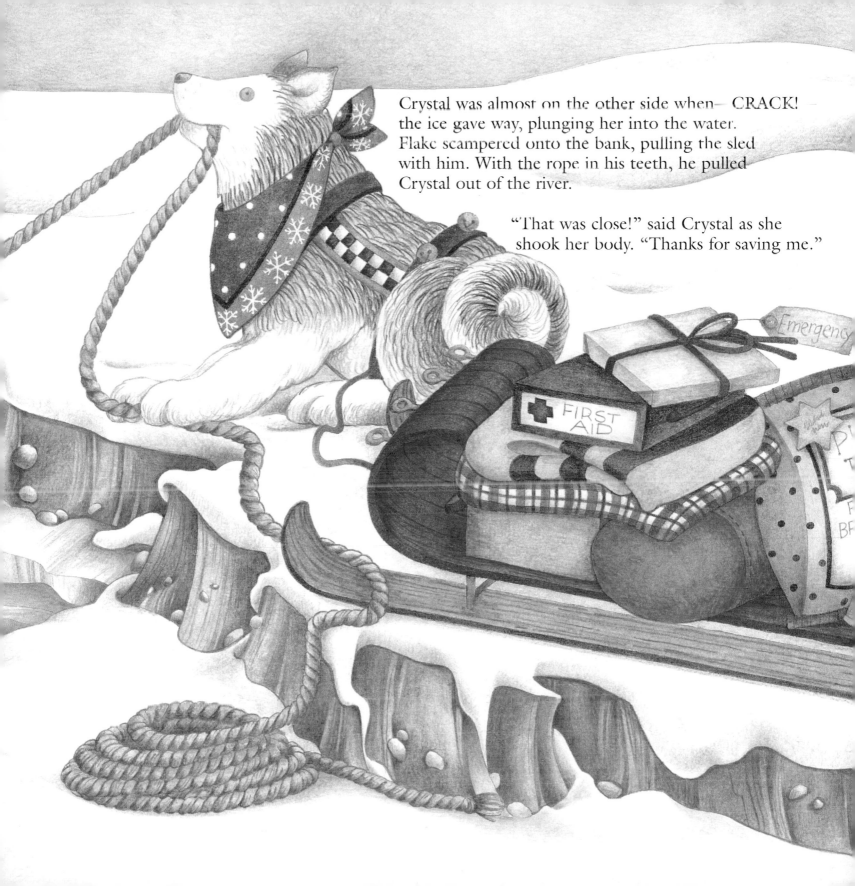

Crystal was almost on the other side when— CRACK!
the ice gave way, plunging her into the water.
Flake scampered onto the bank, pulling the sled
with him. With the rope in his teeth, he pulled
Crystal out of the river.

"That was close!" said Crystal as she
shook her body. "Thanks for saving me."

Late that afternoon, it got much colder. Crystal sniffed the air. "Smells like snow," she said.

Crystal was right. The storm came suddenly, a cold blasting snow that stung their eyes and blotted out the sun. Flake and Crystal dug a hole in the snow beside their sled. Then they curled up together for warmth.

All night long the blizzard howled around them, but the two husky puppies slept safe and warm beneath the snow.

At dawn they dug their way to the surface. Snowdrifts covered the land as far as the eye could see. Their tracks from the day before were gone. Thin clouds hid the sky. The trail was buried beneath the snow.

"Now we are the ones who are lost," worried Flake. "Maybe Elderberry should send someone out to find us! I think we had better open Mummushka's emergency package now."

Crystal said, "We've done okay on our own so far, Flake. Let's stop and think about what to do next."

"You're right," answered Flake. "We should save the package for a real problem."

At that moment, a puff of wind blew away the clouds. "Look!" said Crystal. "I can see lights from a town!" Away they ran.

While Flake and Crystal were looking for them, Mummford and McFinn had been walking, day after day, across the snowy land. "Do you think we'll be home for Christmas?" asked McFinn.

Mummford patted McFinn on the head. He didn't tell his little brother he was concerned too. "If we just keep walking," he said, "I know we'll reach Igloo Village."

The next day Mummford and McFinn arrived in a small town. Everywhere they looked, people were getting ready for the holidays. Holiday music filled the air, and people hurried through the streets with their arms full of packages.

Mummford saw a boy and his mother putting sand into the bottoms of paper bags and then sticking candles into the sand. "We are making luminarias," said the boy. "On Christmas Eve, we light the candles and put the bags along the walkway to our house to welcome our friends. Take one with you as a souvenir."

Mummford nudged McFinn and said, "What do you say, McFinn?"
McFinn blushed and said, "Thank you, and Feliz Navidad!"

McFinn and Mummford met a girl with her father who was carrying candelabra. "Is that a Christmas decoration?" asked Mummford.

"In our family, we celebrate Chanukah with a menorah," said the girl. "We light one candle a day for eight days. We eat potato pancakes and applesauce, and we play spin-the-dreidel." In her hand she held out a wooden top. "Here," she said. "From me to you."
McFinn nudged Mummford. "What do you say, Mummford?"
Mummford blushed. "Thank you, and Happy Chanukah!"

McFinn bumped into a boy carrying red, green, and black candles. "Are those for your menorah?" he asked.

"No," said the boy. "We celebrate Kwanzaa. For seven days we honor our ancestors by lighting the candles in our kinara. We think of ways to make our lives better and to help each other. And we make presents for each other. That's called Kuumba, or being creative. I made the candles for our kinara this year. Take some."

And McFinn and Mummford said, "Thank you, and Happy Kwanzaa!"

As they walked through the town, Mummford and McFinn saw people stringing colored lights on trees and houses. Others were putting candles in windows. Inside the homes people were baking cakes, pies, and cookies.

"Do you think Igloo Village is as ready for the holidays as this town is?" asked McFinn. "I can't wait to get home and tell everyone what we've seen! I never knew there were so many wonderful ways to celebrate this time of year."

Mummford and McFinn came around a corner into the town square. They stopped in their tracks. There stood a magnificent Christmas tree, covered with beautiful lights. At the top shone a glowing, golden star.

"That's beautiful! We should have a Christmas tree in Igloo Village," said Mummford.

McFinn added, "But trees don't grow where we live."

"Then we'll just have to take one home with us!" said Mummford.

Mummford and McFinn found a lovely Christmas tree, and a kind man helped them get it ready to travel. He wrapped the tree with a heavy brown cloth so it would not be hurt by dragging it on the ground.

All day long, Mummford and McFinn pulled their Christmas tree across the snow. It was a big job for two little penguins.

With every passing hour, Mummford felt more and more worried. Soon he would have to tell his little brother that they were lost. They had found a beautiful Christmas tree, but they were not going to get home in time to share it with their family and friends. Maybe they would not get home at all.

McFinn interrupted Mummford's dreary thoughts. "Listen! I hear barking!"

"Hooray," shouted McFinn. "It's Flake and Crystal!" The friends met and hugged and laughed and tumbled in the snow together.

"We're so glad to see you!" said Mummford. "Now we can all go home together."

McFinn said, "We have a tree, a dreidel, some candles, and luminarias! We are ready for Christmas and Chanukah and Kwanzaa, but mostly we are ready to be home!"

Home is the place that always waits for you.

But even with all four of them working to move the sled along, it still looked like they would never get home. Everyone sat down, and little McFinn was ready to cry.

Then remembering the package in brown paper, Crystal said, "Here. Your mother said we should open this in case of an emergency."

Both penguins tore off the paper. Inside was a photograph of everyone in Igloo Village. Mummushka had written on it:

Home is the place that always waits for you.

That little picture was just what the weary friends needed to see. Mummford jumped to his feet. "Who's ready to go home for the holidays?" Everyone shouted, "We are!"

Eagerly they set off again, Flake and Crystal pulling the heavy sled. From that moment on, the snowy trail seemed to go flying past.

All of Igloo Village came out to welcome them. Mummford and McFinn were hugged and kissed and patted and fussed over. The brave huskies were treated like heroes.

Mummford said, "We have brought Igloo Village's first Christmas tree!"

Everyone helped decorate the tree with the dreidel and the candles and colored lights and paper snowflakes, with strings of popcorn and cranberries. They hung a shining star at the top. Then they put lighted luminarias around the tree. It looked magnificent!

Mummford looked at the happy faces of Igloo Village. He smiled and said, "Being at home with our Mummushka and our dear friends is the most wondrous part of the holidays!"